On a tall hill
in a tall house
lived a tall man
and a small mouse.

But the tall man never saw the mouse
and the mouse never saw the man in the house.

What did the tall man do all day?

Well …

he did tall things
that needed doing.

He picked apples,

untangled swings,
whistled songs
he couldn't sing,

rescued cats
and kites from trees,
showed great care
for many things.

And what about the mouse? Well ...

by day she slept
and at night she crept
to do small things
that needed doing:
like finding pins
and pegs and corks,
long, sharp nails
and long-lost forks.
A special pen, a silver ring,
a watch, a coin, a shiny thing.

Afterwards she'd crawl and creep
to find a comfy place to sleep.

ZZZzzzzz

One day
the man went to fix
the town's great clock.
It had no *tick*,
it had no *tock*!

The tall man poked,
he pulled and tied,
prodded, shook,
and then he cried,
"If only I could get inside!"

The tall man tried
and tried
and *tried*.

At last he said,
"What can I do?
I'll have to think up
something new."

And home he went,
without a clue.

The tall man looked
and looked and looked
through every page
of every book,
but he still didn't know
how to fix the clock
which would not *tick*
and would not *tock*.

At the end of the long day
the tall man
took off his long shoes,
wiggled his long toes
and had a long snooze.

ZZZZzzz

Meanwhile, as the
tall man slept …

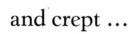

the small mouse crept …

and crept …

and crept.

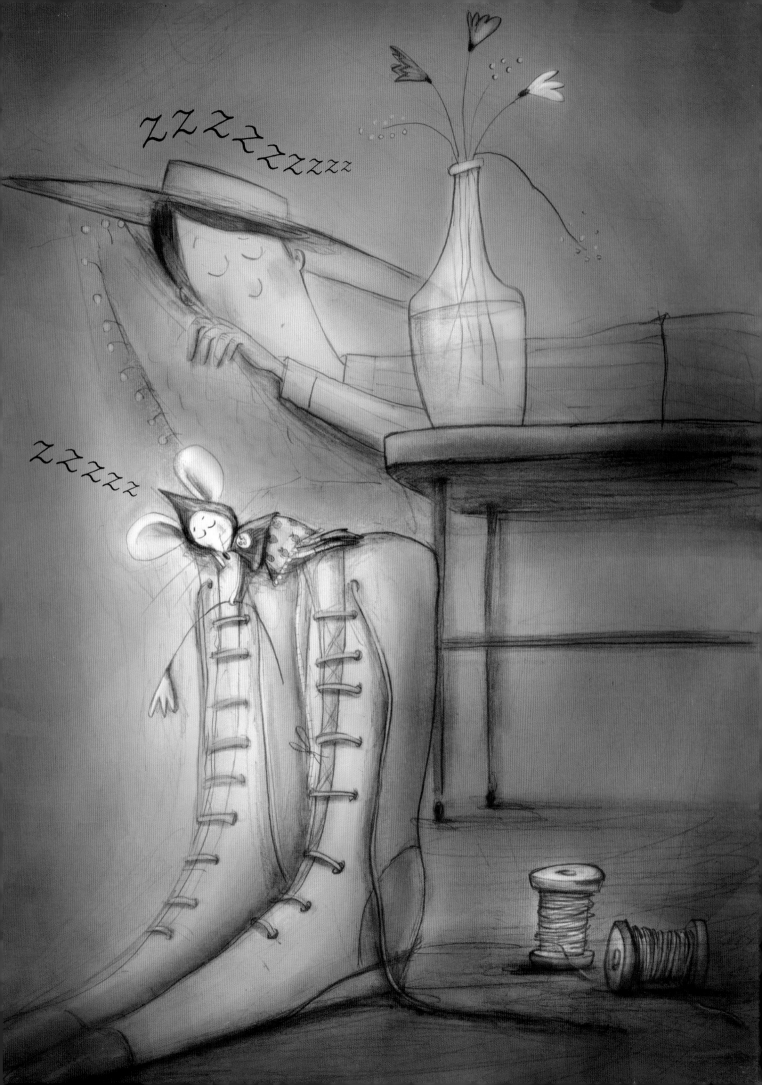

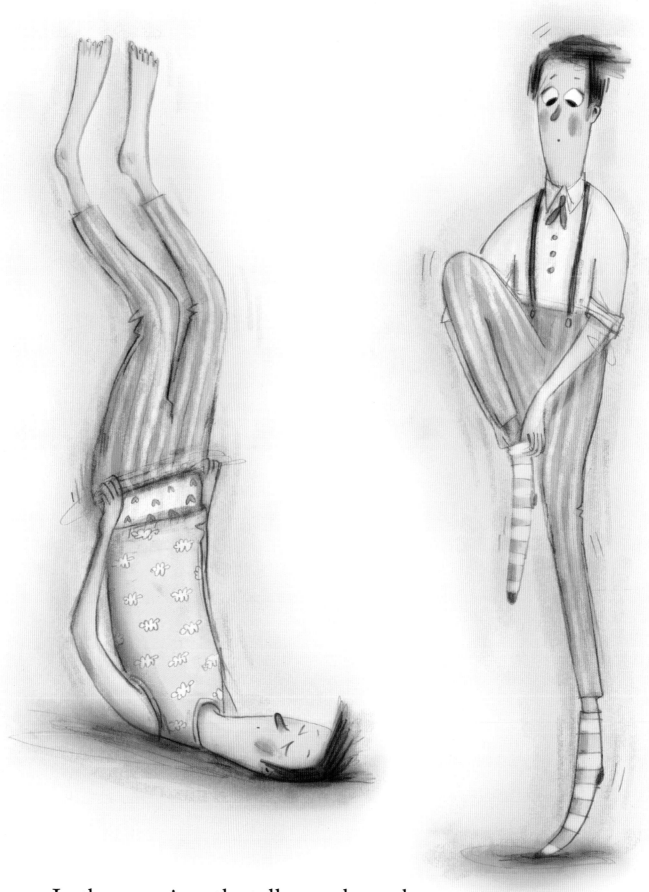

In the morning, the tall man dressed
in the clothes that he liked best

and was putting on his long shoes,
when the small mouse woke and ...

The tall man had a peek – "EEEK!"
He said, "Oh my, I never knew
a mouse was sleeping in my shoe!"

Then he saw all his missing things.
The tall man's heart began to sing!

"Mouse," he said, "you're clearly clever,
small and nimble, I wonder whether
I may possibly borrow you?
I've a most important thing to do."

"Squeak! Squeak! Squeak!"

Down the tall hill
from the tall house
went the tall man
and the small mouse.

In the town's great square
was the town's big clock
which would not *tick*
and would not *tock*.

The mouse was really very small
and in she went to creep and crawl
to search and find that broken thing
for the man to fix
so the clock could *ding*!

But where would she find it
and where should she go?
What did it look like?
The mouse didn't know!

She looked high and low,
she looked here and there,
she looked left and right,
she searched
EVERYWHERE ...

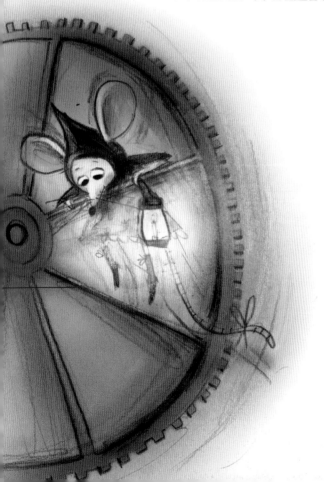

till finally the small mouse saw
the broken thing she was looking for!

"Squeak! Squeak! Squeak!"

The tall man heard the mouse
     and thought,
As she's so small and likes to find
and I'm so tall and like to fix,
together we're the perfect mix!

He said, "And now it's time to try!"

So with string
and a cork,
a coin and a key …

the man and the mouse
fixed the clock. "Yippeeeeee!!"
The tall clock's bells
began to ring,
and both their hearts
began to sing.

The tall man said,
"We may be two of a different kind,
but both of us can fix and find.
I'm your friend and you are mine."

"Squeak! Squeak! Squeak!"

On a tall hill
in a tall house
live a tall man
and a small mouse.

What do the two friends do all day?

Well ...

come rain or shine, whatever the weather,
they do the things that need doing
TOGETHER.